GOING FOR BROKE

MEG McKINLAY

WALKER
BOOKS

First published in Great Britain 2009 by Walker Books Ltd
87 Vauxhall Walk, London SE11 5HJ

2 4 6 8 10 9 7 5 3 1

This book has been typeset in Frutiger

Printed and bound in Great Britain by Clays Ltd, St Ives plc

British Library Cataloguing in Publication Data:
a catalogue record for this book is
available from the British Library

ISBN 978-1-4063-2214-9

www.walker.co.uk

For James and Thomas, record-breaking nephews

CHAPTER 1
DORKFACE GETS A PLAN

It's Josh Tuttle dropping his trophy on my foot at the end-of-term assembly that finally makes my mind up.

It's not all his fault, though. He's just the last straw, the last amazing genius in an assembly full of kids doing fantastic, unbelievable things.

Apart from being so all-round wonderful and talented, these kids all have one thing in common.

They are not me.

The official theme for the assembly is "Young Achievers", but it might as well be "Everyone In This

School Is Way Better Than You, Dork-Face".

First, it's Janie Parsons and her robotic dog. That thing can roll over, beg, and fetch a newspaper. It's a marvel of modern science, built entirely from tin cans and parts from a radio she found at the rubbish tip.

Mr Stipanov, the principal, applauds so hard he almost falls over. Then he gives Janie a little crystal ball on a gold stand. She's a Young Scientist of the New Millennium.

Next, it's Anthony Jenkovic and his black belt in every martial art you've ever heard of. And some you haven't. Which I suspect he might have actually made up himself.

Mr Stipanov fake karate chops him, and hands him a shiny plaque in the shape of a clenched fist, covered in Japanese writing. Anthony, he says, is a Butt Kicker for the Modern Age.

Okay, he doesn't exactly say that. But that's what he means.

Then it's maths geniuses and junior sports stars and kids who play chess on weekends. There's even a Year One kid who scored a part in *Neighbours*. His job is to point at a sports car and say "Coool!" The whole school goes wild for him. Girls in Year Seven want his autograph.

The kid is six years old. He probably doesn't even know how to write. For all I know, it took him twenty-seven takes to get that one word right. For all I know, they ended up dubbing it in later.

It doesn't matter. He's a star.

And I'm sitting on my bum on a piece of ratty carpet square while Year Seven kids flick spitballs at me from behind.

Finally, it's Josh Tuttle, breaking the State Record for the 800 metres. He fist-pumps the air as he walks up to collect a trophy that's almost as tall as he is.

I clap along with everyone else, because Mrs Cheval is watching, then I turn to Weasel Burton, who's grinding his teeth next to me.

"Is it just me," I say, "or are there way too many high achievers at this school?"

Weasel grins, and jabs me in the side again. So

far, he's managed to wind me five times without Mrs Cheval noticing once.

Now *that's* talent.

I shuffle my bum around on my piece of carpet; it's so frayed it hardly keeps me off the cold concrete now. But that's probably because I spend every assembly picking at the loose threads when I'm bored, which is all the time.

There's only so much basking in other people's glory you can take.

At least this one's nearly over. All that's left is for Mr Stipanov to make a short speech about the amazing amazingness of all the kids lined up on the stage. He'll say "Well, children" and "real credit to the school" about sixteen times. Then the photographer from the local paper will take photos and write an article about the incredible talent and skill of all the kids who aren't me.

Shouldn't be long now.

Oh, wait.

There's one more thing.

"*Well, children*, it seems that last assembly we left one student, who is also a *real credit to the school*, out of the merit awards."

This is *terribly unfortunate*, apparently. Mr Stipanov is falling over himself to apologise.

Weasel digs me in the ribs again, snickering. According to Mr Stipanov, some "cheerful lad" has won a small rectangle of red cardboard for being "a kind-hearted and thoughtful classmate".

Sucked in to that kid.

Last year, I won mine for "writing a very interesting narrative recount". Go ahead, ask me. I have no idea what a narrative recount is. I did write a note to Weasel about the time Dad backed the car into a tree, so maybe that was it.

The point is, it doesn't matter. Everyone knows you win one merit award a year, no matter how much you suck. You could sit in a corner farting all year and they'd still find something for you.

CERTIFICATE OF MERIT

awarded to

Wendell Burton

for Consistent Commitment
To Gas Production
Wendell Is A Conscientious
Consumer Of Baked Beans.
Keep up the good work, Wendell!

Mrs Cheval

There's a scattering of no-one-really-cares applause and then someone pokes me in the side.

"Go on!"

I look up from picking at my carpet square. From the non-Weasel side, Ronnie Symons is waggling his eyebrows, and Mrs Cheval is leaning down the row, hissing at me.

That's when I play back Mr Stipanov's announcement in my head, and my whole body goes cold.

" … this extra special end-of-term assembly merit award goes to … Nathan Foley."

Being me.

Ronnie and Weasel push me forward and I stumble up and out of the line, and start the long, slow march down the centre of the aisle. I keep my eyes focused on Mr Stipanov and his tiny square of red cardboard, and try not to be blinded by the flashes of gold and polished metal behind him on the stage.

Mr Stipanov leans forward, beaming, and shakes my hand. "Well done, son. Nothing like being a cheerful lad."

I turn to walk back to my place, but he waves me up onto the stage "with our other prize-winners". I squeeze in next to Josh Tuttle, my craptacular square of cardboard behind my back, and that's when it happens.

They should have seen it coming, really. Because Josh Tuttle, in spite of all his amazing amazingness, is not that big. He's one of those wiry, zippy guys who slips past you in a race like the air's opening up to let him through. He's the guy you don't see coming until he's whizzed past your ear.

As I watch him lose his grip on the trophy, and see it toppling towards me, I think how much better it would have been if they'd just given him a square of cardboard.

The edge of the trophy's base comes down hard on my foot.

A camera flashes, catching me mid-*auuuughhhh!*, and this is the picture that will appear in the school newsletter tomorrow. If you look closely at my flailing hands, you'll be able to make out the smiley-face stickers on my merit award.

I stumble backwards into the row of kids behind me. Luckily, they're all legends of martial arts and various other sports, and they brace themselves against me, blocking my fall.

From the wings, Mr Marshall, the caretaker, lunges onto the stage and grabs the trophy. He pulls it back towards him, using my foot as a pivot point.

In the crowd, Ronnie and Weasel are grinning, doing a long, slow handclap all on their own.

Mr Marshall glares at me, and escorts Josh to the other end of the row. For the rest of the assembly, he acts as Josh's own personal trophy-holder.

"I think my toe is broken," I say, to no one in particular.

"Shut up, Foley," replies someone behind me, so I do. I stand there with my throbbing toe, my square of red cardboard shoved into my back pocket. I'll get in trouble for that later, when it's time for the newspaper journalist to smirk and put me in the centre of his "junior champions" photo spread, but I'm not thinking about that now.

I'm watching Weasel point at me and mouth the word "high achiever" over and over while silently cacking himself.

And I'm working out a foolproof, ingenious plan for becoming amazingly amazing. For getting up on stage, in the paper even, without a broken toe and a really lame square of red cardboard.

CHAPTER 2
SERIOUS-LOOKING RAMP

When I announce my plan after school, Weasel and Ronnie stare at me and shake their heads.

"You can't just suddenly get famous, you know," Weasel says. "You have to be *good* at something."

"Yeah," Ronnie adds. "You have to have an actual, you know, skill."

"Not true," I say. "Check this out."

We're sitting on the grass on the far side of the oval, our bikes in a tangled heap next to us. I reach into my backpack and pull out the book:

AMAZING
WORLD RECORDS

UNMATCHABLE FEATS!
INCREDIBLE FACTS!

The cover is a collage of tiny photos, and Ronnie's finger falls on what looks like a chicken with a deformed head. He raises his eyebrows. I turn the cover quickly and flip through the pages.

"Longest hair," I read. "Loudest scream."

Weasel looks over my shoulder. "Hang on," he says. "Fastest *furniture*?"

There's a picture of a guy in goggles riding a sofa. It's got some kind of rocket-type thing strapped to the back.

"That's cool!" Weasel says. "Hey, the junk collection's coming up. We could score some stuff, easy. Then all we'd need is an engine. Maybe we could talk to Janie Parsons?" He looks up at me. "She could probably whip something up out of pipe-cleaners in no time."

I shake my head and flip through another chunk of pages.

"Most consecutive number of football passes," I say.

"Most scorpions eaten," offers Weasel.

"Longest yodel," I say, turning away from the *Dangerous Animals* section.

"Sharing a bathtub with the most rattlesnakes," says Ronnie, turning back.

"Is it just me," I say, "or are you trying to kill me?"

Weasel leans back on his elbows. "We're just trying to find something you might actually be able to do. It's not our fault they all involve poisonous animals."

A picture catches my eye, then. A bike, a ramp, a maniac in a helmet.

CATEGORY: AMAZING FEATS
RECORD: LONGEST AIRBORNE JUMP BY
BICYCLE

"Aha!" I tap the photo with my finger, and check out the caption.

LUCAS NELSON, 16

He's an average-looking kid – brown hair, freckles, not too tall or too short. He doesn't look that amazingly amazing.

"I could do that," I say.

"You reckon?"

"It's a bike," I say. "It's a jump."

Weasel leans in and examines the picture. Then he looks at me and grins.

"Up the bush?" he says.

I nod. We've been jumping our bikes up there for years, off piles of gravel and the edges of shallow gullies. We've never built an actual ramp, but it looks easy enough.

Ronnie pulls the book over and peers at it. "Serious-looking ramp," he says. "Serious-looking bike."

He glances doubtfully at my bike, with its busted spokes, bent handlebars, and rusted rims.

I jump up. "Nah, it'll be cool. We just have to build a ramp. There's heaps of junk up in the bush, old wood and stuff."

I look at the picture again. There's no second ramp – it's just Lucas and his bike midair. Ronnie shakes his head again.

"You just stack it," I say. "At the end. It doesn't matter. It's not like I've never stacked it before. It's the distance that counts."

Oh, yeah, the distance. Small detail. How far was that, exactly?

TWELVE METRES.

**NOTE: RAMP TO BE NO HIGHER THAN 1.6 METRES, NO LONGER THAN TEN. TOTAL RUN-UP OF NO LONGER THAN TWENTY METRES.

"This is getting kind of technical." Ronnie frowns and flips to the next page. "Here you go – world's biggest bicycle. World's *smallest* bicycle." He looks up. "That sounds a lot safer. Possible, even. You just have to build stuff."

"Who do you think I am?" I say. "Janie Parsons?

I don't want to build something; I want to *do* something. Anyway, didn't you want me to take a bath with rattlesnakes? Now you're telling me the *bike's* too dangerous?"

"I'm just saying ..." Ronnie scratches his head. "There's heaps of stuff in here. Tallest boy, longest hair, largest quantity of bellybutton fluff ..."

I shake my head. "No way."

"Airborne jump," Weasel says. "Tomorrow."

"Bring your mum's video camera, Ronnie," I say. "We'd better film it. You know, for proof."

Weasel nods. "Yeah, good thinking." Then he turns quickly. "Time to go, boys."

Mr Marshall's coming across the oval towards us, yelling something. He's too far away to hear properly, but we know what it is:

Get out of here, you kids. No hanging around on school property after hours.

I check my watch. The term ended exactly thirty-two minutes ago.

Mr Marshall takes his job way too seriously.

Weasel pulls his bike out of the pile and jumps on, wobbling the front wheel across the grass.

"Race ya!"

I glance at Ronnie, but he shakes his head. "I have to get home," he says. "I'll see you tomorrow."

I nod.

"Here. You better take this."

He goes to pass me the book, but it slips from his hands. As I bend to pick it up, I see the page it's fallen open to. There's Lucas Nelson, 16, staring out at me again, his bike aimed forward like an arrow.

Like a challenge.

I slam the book shut and shove it back into my bag. Then I grab my bike, give the wheel a kick to stop it rubbing against the frame, and take off after Weasel.

CHAPTER 3
THE AMAZING NATHAN

"I don't think this is going to work." Weasel takes a step back and frowns.

The milk crates we dragged off the dump look dangerously wobbly. Somehow, Weasel and I overlooked some of the details when we were drawing diagrams and scouting for junk yesterday. In our plan, the crates just sit there, slotting neatly into each other.

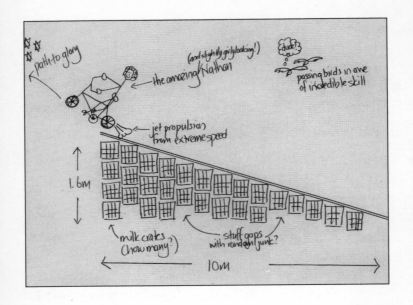

In reality, we've had to dig them into the ground with old tent pegs Ronnie brought with him, then tie them together with his ockie straps.

In reality, the whole thing looks totally bodgy and almost as death-defying as getting into a bathtub full of rattlesnakes.

Weasel scratches his head. "Maybe we need a welding iron or something?"

Ronnie snorts. "For *plastic*? Good thinking." He turns to me. "You sure about this, Nath? It looks–"

I pick up a tent peg and head for the ramp. "Nah, it'll be fine."

Once you've come this far, you can't just turn around and go home. Once you've got half a ramp built, you can't take it apart and pretend you didn't really care anyway.

I lean the wood up against the crates and turn to Ronnie. "How are we going to make this thing stay?"

He sighs. "You guys thought of everything, didn't you?"

We can't do it with ockie straps, because then I'll have to ride over them and that'll slow me down. I need maximum speed; I need a flawless run-up.

I bet Lucas Nelson didn't have to deal with ockie straps.

Come to think of it … I take the book out of my bag and flip to the right page. How did they make that thing? It looks like the sort of ramp you see on stunt shows. Like he had a professional team or something, a whole pit crew behind the scenes.

There's a crashing sound behind me and I turn

to find Weasel lying flat on his face on a sheet of plywood.

"I thought we could use one more piece," he says, clutching his side. "I just tripped. I'm okay."

It figures. Lucas Nelson, Boy Wonder, has a whole pit crew of streamlined professionals and I have these two.

I glance at Ronnie, who's hard at work on something next to me.

"I dunno if this is gonna hold it." He flips the bottle in his hand over to read the directions on the back.

- **Squeeze gently**
- **Press surfaces together and clamp tightly**
- **Always ask an adult for help**
- **Perfect for paper, card and fabric!**

Oh, good.

He's trying to use craft glue to attach the plywood ramp to the milk crates.

We are all class.

"Maybe we could make the ramp out of pipe-cleaners," I mutter. "That's about all that glue's good for."

Ronnie snaps the lid back on. "I told you this was a stupid idea. Anyway, without me you wouldn't even have the crates stuck together." He leans across to get a closer look at the book. "Check this out. Hey, did you even read this?" He trails his finger down the lines next to the photo.

LUCAS AND HIS FATHER, PROFESSIONAL STUNTMAN DARYL NELSON, SHOW THEIR STYLE

Oops.

He shoves the book back at me. "*Professional stuntman*! And you want to build this out of milk crates and old wood from the tip?" He jabs a finger at the edge of the photo, where what looks suspiciously like the very tip of a second ramp – a landing ramp? – is jutting into the frame. "And I reckon–"

Weasel winces suddenly, grabbing his leg. "*Splintery* old wood from the tip."

He glances down at the book. It's got a ding in the spine and a couple of green streaks on the cover from when it landed on the grass yesterday. The two pages about Lucas Nelson are stuck together from the glue Ronnie had on his fingers.

"Are you even supposed to have this out?" Weasel says. "Isn't it a reference book or something?"

"Sort of."

Ronnie rolls his eyes. "You should have got one of the older ones. It's only the new one you can't borrow."

"Oh yeah. Good idea," I reply. "So we end up breaking a record that's already been broken two years ago."

Weasel grins. "Might give us a better chance, though."

"Yeah." Ronnie runs a finger along the glue-splattered wood. "I reckon if we went way back, maybe all the way back to the days of the penny-farthing bike, we might be in with a shot. Given the quality of our equipment."

"And our pit crew."

"Guys." Weasel looks thoughtful. "I reckon …"

He picks up the second sheet of wood again and motions to us to help him position it on top of the crates. We lower it down between the three of us, and move it around until it's roughly centred.

"I reckon," he goes on, "if me and Ronnie can just hold the wood while you go up, the weight of the bike will help keep it on." He looks across at me. "As long as you stay in the middle. But you need to, anyway. If you start zigging and zagging, you'll lose speed. So it's all good. Maybe."

Ronnie looks down at the wood. "We just hold it?"

"Yep." Weasel crouches down on one side and presses a hand to each side of the wood, sandwiching it steady. "If you do that side, it'll be sweet." He looks down. "Just don't run over my fingers."

When we've stacked enough crates, I take the bike up to the edge of the gully. From here, I can start my downhill run-up, pick up some speed before I hit the edge of the ramp.

That's my theory.

With Weasel and Ronnie holding the sloping wood against the crates, I hoon down the hill towards the ramp, my wheels throwing up tiny stones all around me. I keep my head down, and in the corner of my eye I see Weasel inch to the side, a panicked look on his face as I fly towards him.

It's a bit of a worry, actually. The wood looked really wide when we were putting it on. From here, it looks different. It looks narrow, and bodgy, and kind of … impossible.

The front wheel crunches off the ground and onto the ramp. It's a sharp angle, and there's a thump. The back spins out a bit and I lose some speed. I jump up off the seat to get it back, pulling on the pedals. Then I'm flying, up towards the top, towards the edge, and Weasel yells "Wahoo!" My head snaps up and for a split second I have a premium view of old rusting car bodies and broken furniture.

Ronnie's running next to me with the camera and the measuring tape, and then the ramp runs out and I'm in the air. I'm going and going, remembering only at the last second that I'm meant to aim the bike like an arrow instead of jerking it backwards and forwards like a lunatic, and then I'm falling and falling.

I brace myself for the impact, and just before I hit the ground it occurs to me that we should probably have cleared a path here, that rusting car bodies and broken furniture aren't the softest landing. And then I'm down, the bike's landing cushioned by a mouldy old sofa, my own landing not so cushioned by the bike and the sofa springs sticking up through its frame.

For a second, I'm paralysed, every bone screaming. I'm wishing I'd made myself a nice comfy landing ramp. Then I'm realising my chances of actually landing on it would have probably been about zero.

I untangle myself and sit up.

Weasel's back near the ramp, shaking his head and grinning.

Ronnie's next to the sofa, shaking his head and frowning. "Six metres," he says. "You need to get way higher."

"*Six*?"

"Hey." Weasel runs up. "It's not bad for a first try." He starts shifting junk out of the way. "Should probably have thought of this before, yeah?"

"Yeah." I rub my knee, which is already a patchy purple colour.

Ronnie looks down at the tape again. "You guys. I reckon we can't just do this. We need to plan it better. We need to, like, plot it out, you know? Use the laws of physics or something."

Weasel snorts. "Laws of physics? Oh yeah, and what would they be, Science Boy?"

Ronnie shrugs. "We could find out."

I kick the front wheel to straighten it back out. "I'm going again."

The second attempt is faster, and higher, and further. The landing is also less life-threatening, now Weasel's removed all the sharp objects from my path.

"See," I say. "It's just practice."

I am developing quiet confidence and a steely gaze. I have Lucas Nelson and his superhero father firmly in my sights.

The third attempt is when it all falls apart.

Coming off my run-up, I'm going fast. Faster than before, and I get some air as I come off the dirt onto the ramp. Just a bit, but it's enough. Enough to expose the fundamental design flaw.

I feel the plywood start to splinter as the front wheel comes down, and my brain has time to think this:

Uh-oh … no, wait, it's okay, cos I'm going fast. I'll stay ahead of the split, see, I've already gone past it … uh-oh, the split is following me, the wheel is making the split, the whole thing is cracking … okay, so the wood's cracked, but the crates are okay, I'll just slow down and stop … nice and easy …

Or not.

I'm right. The crates are fine.

What I forget is that there are gaps between the crates. We didn't have enough so we had to space them out. But it didn't matter, because the wood was strong. It would hold, no problem.

That's what Science Boy reckoned.

The front wheel crashes down into the gap, and I follow it. The back of the bike sticks straight up for a second, then flips over the front, with me underneath it. My head hits the splintered wood, the handlebars, and the edge of a milk crate. Then it hits the ground, and the bike lands on top of me, bringing more cracking wood with it.

Ronnie and Weasel rush over, and I'm about to tell them I'm okay, in case I actually am, but then Weasel grabs the measuring tape and stretches it out alongside me.

"What's that?" he says. "Minus a metre? Two? Can you get a *negative* world record?"

"Shut up," I groan, "and pass me the stupid book."

CHAPTER 4
SO CLOSE, MATE

"How about world's most *mangled* bike?" Weasel breaks a twisted spoke off the wheel and jabs it at me like a sword.

"I told you we needed to aim a bit lower," Ronnie says, flipping through the book.

"Lower?" Weasel laughs. "How? You think he should actually *eat* the dirt?"

Ronnie sighs. "You know what I mean. Easier. Less spectacular. Here."

He pushes the book towards me, tapping the

middle of the page. It's a few lines and a small photo, about the size of a stamp. Not exactly the double-page Lucas Nelson spread. And I can't make out what it is – there's a guy's head there somewhere, but it's almost completely hidden by a big white thing; actually, the whole picture is dotted with little white flecks. Then I see the heading:

CATEGORY: AMAZING FEATS
RECORD: FASTEST ONION-EATING

I raise my eyebrows. It's a picture of a man, a large vegetable, and a whole world of spit. "Are you serious?"

Weasel pokes at the picture with the spoke. "Mate, you are *not* doing that."

"No, I'm not."

Ronnie looks meaningfully at my grazed leg and the bump on my head. I ignore him meaningfully right back.

"I was getting there," I say. I look at Weasel. "I was getting there, wasn't I?"

Weasel snaps the measuring tape back into its

holder. "Kind of. Seven and a half metres. It's over halfway."

"Yeah." Ronnie snorts. "All we need now is a new ramp, a new bike and a professional stuntman to get us through the next half. So close, mate."

Weasel stares at the ramp. "Hang on," he says. He takes the book and finds Lucas again, then flips a couple of pages back. "Yeah!"

"What?" I pull myself up to a sitting position.

Ronnie shakes his head. "No way."

"It's perfect." Weasel thrusts the book towards me. "No building. No craft glue. No splintering wood."

He's pointing at a photo of a kid on a skateboard. A little kid, wiry, Josh Tuttle-style. He's crouching like a cat on the board, knees bent, arms splayed out to the sides, surfing a railing.

A long one.

"Forty-six metres."

"That's not that long."

Ronnie nods his head at the wreckage. "Yeah? It's nearly four times as long as your mate Lucas."

Weasel grabs the book. "It's totally different. It's a *skateboard*, on a *rail*." He turns to me. "The railing at school. You know."

Yeah. That railing. The one that runs the whole length of the school, all the way from the office right down to the canteen. One long, continuous railing.

Ronnie frowns. "Aren't there, like, corners and downhill bits and ..."

Weasel grins. "Easy," he says. "We'll work it out."

"Do you even know how to skateboard?" Ronnie shields his eyes against the glare off the rusty metal around us and stares at me.

"Does he know how to skateboard?" Weasel answers for me. "Anyone can skateboard, mate. All you need is balance."

CHAPTER 5
ANYONE CAN SKATEBOARD

"Mate." Weasel stares down at me, shaking his head.

"Balance," says Ronnie. "It's all about balance."

The good news is, I've actually made it a fair way.

The good news is, I do much better with something underneath me instead of just air.

The good news is, there's no spiky furniture here to puncture me when I crash.

Because I do. Crash.

The bad news is, Weasel's theory was wrong.

Balance isn't the only thing you need. You also

need half a clue. You need lots of practice. You need a really thick skin and flexible bones.

So I crash, a lot. Ronnie was right. There are downhill bits and corners. Two nasty corners that wrap the rail around B-Block, just down the steepest part of the hill. If I make the first one, I stack it spectacularly on the second. If I stack it spectacularly on the first one, I don't get to the second one. I haven't made it anywhere near the canteen yet, not even close.

Weasel isn't much help.

Remember he said it was easy, that we'd work it out?

What he meant was, he'd put me on a skateboard, mumble something about the laws of physics, and give me a push.

It's not exactly science.

I pick myself up from the concrete and tuck the board under one arm. It's still in one piece, which is good, because it means I can go again, after we solve our little cornering problem.

Weasel looks the railing up and down. "I dunno ...

it doesn't *look* that tight." He turns to Ronnie. "Don't suppose you've got any ideas, Science Boy?"

"Don't look at me." Ronnie holds up his hands. "I voted for the onion, remember?"

Weasel frowns. "You need to go faster," he says. "Or maybe slower. Hang on."

He flips the book open and points at a photo. It's a guy cornering on a ramp, doing a 180 in the air.

"I'm not jumping," I say, rubbing the bump on my head.

Weasel laughs. "Nah. Might work though." He looks thoughtful. "Nah. I just mean ..." He taps the picture. "See."

It's like the board is glued to the guy's feet, like he's sucked it up towards himself. He's bent in the middle, his knees drawn up to his stomach, his elbows in tight against his sides.

He's like a flying piano accordion, mid-squeeze.

"You just gotta stay low." Weasel nods like he knows what he's talking about. "You have to do that crouching thing. Bend your knees."

I look at the picture again. Stay low. Bend my knees. Yeah. I can do that.

I put the board down and step onto it, practise folding myself up and down. It's easy. It's like surfing. Like pictures of other people surfing. Which I've seen.

"No worries."

I pace myself. I'm not stupid. Not since the sofa spring incident, anyway.

I practise on the path near the office, twisting and turning on the ground, where it's nice and safe and there isn't far to fall. I bend my knees and crouch down, and it feels good. Weasel was right. It's easier this way. I climb up onto the railing and try it on the corner of the building. It's not as tight as the others, but it's close, and I make it, no problem.

I try again, and I nail it. Over and over.

Easy.

Weasel jumps to his feet. "You're ready, mate. Let's go."

I'm going to do this. I can feel it.

He smiles and punches me in the shoulder.

Ronnie trails along behind us. "You should practise down there." He points at B-Block. "Just do the actual corners once, off the downhill. Before you go at it like a maniac again. It's steep, you know."

I ignore him and climb onto the rail. I set the board down in front of me and start to roll. It feels good, steady. I experiment as I go, crouching low every now and then to pick up speed. Once I'm going fast enough, I don't even wobble; I just surf the railing down and down. Weasel and Ronnie run along beside me, yelling.

When I reach the first corner, I'm flying. The rail angles around in front of me and I lean forward into it, the board suckering itself to my feet like a second skin. Then I think piano accordion, press the soles of my feet to the board, and get low.

There's a moment of lift-off. I'm sure there is. Just a split second when I'm actually in the air, and then gravity takes over. There's no time to think about it, to tell myself, *hey, I'm doing it*. I'm just doing it. The front of the board comes down hard onto the other side of the corner, the weight of my feet clamping it down firmly.

"Yeah!" Weasel fist-pumps the air, and then I'm off again, rolling.

Heading for the second corner.

"Hey!" Ronnie runs to catch up. "One corner, remember? Practise first? There's—"

I don't hear the rest of it because I'm flying – not slowing down, not interested.

Weasel's jogging backwards just ahead of me, grinning. He knows I'm not stopping. Once you start flying, why would you stop to be sensible?

The second one's going to be harder. I haven't got the speed I had coming off the slope, and I'm still getting my rhythm back after the first one. For a second, I think Ronnie was right. One corner, and then a break. Pause to reflect on your achievement. Draw some diagrams. Have a nice cup of tea.

Nah.

I lean forward and stay low. It's tricky, and I almost lose it, but it works. I pick up speed as I roll down the flat and by the time I reach the second corner, I'm flying again.

I'm halfway round – further than I've ever made it – when I realise this one is different. It doesn't just curve around; it kind of wiggles, to get around a big pipe stuck to the side of the building.

Just stay up, I tell myself. *Deal with the rest later.*

It's the same as all those practice runs, isn't it? *Bend your knees. Stay low.*

Yeah. This is where it would be good if I knew how to balance. I follow the wiggles, leaning this way and that. I'm all over the place and the board's getting ahead of me, the front of it tipping up as the rail straightens out and starts to run downhill again.

CLUNK!

The board slams back down. An electric jolt shoots up through my legs all the way to my head. My teeth rattle like loose bones in my mouth, and I taste blood.

My arms are all over the place, and my back arches in and out as I fight to get stable.

"Get down!" Weasel yells, and I react without thinking.

Almost instantly, the wobble stops. I'm on again. I'm okay. But now I'm picking up speed. Classroom windows whiz past me in a blur. For a second I see the road, the trees, and then it's building again. C-Block. Home of Josh Tuttle and his amazing amazingness.

If school was on now, he'd be sitting in there doing something mind-numbingly boring. Something no one would ever give him a trophy for. I could flip him a nice big wave as I rocketed past on my way to a world record.

If only I had the balance.

"Focus!" yells Weasel as I wobble in towards the windows. It's a wall of glass. If I run into it at this speed, I'll be pizza.

"Fall backwards!" Ronnie calls helpfully.

"No! Don't fall!" Weasel screams, punching Ronnie in the arm.

"Ow! I just meant–"

I don't hear the rest, because I'm getting ahead

of them now as the railing heads down and down, towards the canteen. I wonder how many metres I've done. I wonder how close I am to the record. I raise my head slightly and look ahead, to look at the rail, to see how far there is to go.

That's when I see the corner.

Would you call it a corner?

It's more like a hairpin bend. Just ahead of me, the rail angles in sharply towards the wall of the canteen building in a crazy zigzag.

There's no way I can make that.

And there's no way I can stop.

I come off the end doing some serious speed. I suck the board up towards me and keep my head down. I'm going to stack, spectacularly.

And there's something else.

It's a blur in front of me, below me, but there's something ... a pile of stuff. Metal. Long, black, spiky.

I'm going to land right in the middle of it. I'm dead. Or at least impaled.

Ronnie and Weasel are yelling in my ears.

"Stop!"

"Keep going!"

"Look out!"

"Get down!"

"Fall backwards!"

This is the moment when I wish there was a mouldy old couch to cushion my landing.

Somehow, I manage to stay upright. The board hits the ground beneath me, and stops dead in a pile of what my brain recognises suddenly as tools – screwdrivers, pliers, a shovel. I'm flipped forward in the air and land hard on the grass. And something else.

Something's underneath me, digging into my back. Am I impaled? Is this one of those deals where you're okay until you move but as soon as you do your guts fall out?

Weasel pulls up next to me, panting.

"I'm okay," I say, but then I realise he's not listening. He's focused on something at his feet. He reaches down and I feel something pulling underneath me.

"Oww!"

The lump is gone from my back, and my guts seem to be intact. I look up at Weasel, who's holding something in his hand, grinning.

"Cool!" he says. "A welding iron!"

Ronnie comes up behind him, the camera angled down towards me.

"Turn that thing off!" I say, putting my hand up in front of my face.

Ronnie looks me up and down and shakes his head. "Wouldn't it be easier just to get a walk-on part in *Neighbours*?"

I pull myself up onto my elbows. "Coool!" I say weakly.

"Perfect!" says Weasel. "Can I have your autograph?"

Before I can answer, a shape comes thundering around the corner of the building.

It's Mr Marshall. He's got a hammer in one hand and a crowbar in the other. And he doesn't look happy.

"What are you kids doing?" he yells.

Ronnie and Weasel edge backwards. I'd follow them, but my legs aren't working yet.

"Mr Marshall," Ronnie stammers. "We were just ..."

"Give me that!" Mr Marshall lunges for the welding iron, snatching it out of Weasel's hands. "What do you think you're ..."

He looks down at the skateboard, which has a long gash down the middle and jagged splinters sticking out from it. Then he looks at the railing, and me, still splayed out on the grass.

"You could have killed yourself," he growls.

Ronnie takes a step back behind Weasel, using him as a shield.

"Get out of here! You know you're not supposed to be on school property."

None of us feels like arguing. Ronnie stuffs the camera under his jacket, and he and Weasel turn and run back up the steps. I pull myself up painfully, grab what's left of the board and stagger slowly after them.

CHAPTER 6
LESS DEATH-DEFYING, OR WHATEVER

"I thought you said no splintering wood." I drop the board onto the grass.

Weasel shrugs. "Yeah. Well. How could I know you were going to do such a spectacular stack?"

"We should have checked it out first." I pick dirt out of the graze on my arm. "So stupid."

Ronnie scoffs. "The whole thing was stupid! I told you – you have to practise for ages to do something like that."

"I don't know." Weasel snaps a stick between his

fingers. "You were close. If you'd got to the end, you would have done it."

"Yeah, all you had to do was another twelve metres of railing, half of which actually runs *uphill*."

Ronnie flashes the camera at me, with the frame stilled on Mr Marshall. Behind him, you can see the rail running up the canteen ramp onto the verandah.

Weasel blinks. "It's a gentle slope," he says quickly. "He would've made it."

I groan and lean back on my elbows. Every muscle in my body screams when I move, like a building has fallen on me.

"Anyway, it doesn't matter now. My skateboard's stuffed."

Weasel hurls a piece of stick across the grass. "You could borrow mine, give it another go."

"I don't know," I say. "I reckon that last bit's impossible anyway." I rub my elbow. "I reckon ..." I glance at Ronnie quickly. I don't want to say it. "Maybe we should try something easier. Less death-defying, or whatever."

Ronnie reaches into his pocket and pulls out something large and round. He holds it up to the light as if it were a precious jewel. "Behold the onion!" he says. "How it is safe. And round. And really unlikely to splinter and leave big slivers of wood in your bum."

Weasel stares at Ronnie. Then he leans across and grabs the onion out of his hand. He winds up his bowling arm and lets it go, straight into the big gum tree behind us.

I duck, expecting the onion to shatter and spray juice everywhere, but it just bounces back and falls to the ground with a dull thud.

Ronnie runs across and picks it up. He stands over me, resting it in the palm of one hand.

"Behold the onion!" he says again. "How it laughs in the face of danger. How it will wait, patiently, until its time comes. As it will."

Weasel drops down next to me with the book. He opens it to the first page of the index, which is now covered in scribbled pencil.

Amazing Feats

Longest Airborne Jump by Bicycle

try again with different ramp?

Most Sheep Shorn in 24 hours

hard to get sheep. also shearing things

Longest Rail by Skateboard

next year? watch out for welding irons!

Most Cockroaches Eaten

??? bike shed??

Travel and Transport

Fastest Furniture

mower from the bush?

Longest Barrel Roll

??? wheelie bin

Most Parachute Jumps in 24 Hours

Longest Journey by Tractor

too boring. also, no tractor

Fastest 50 Metres by Milk-bottle Raft

??ockie straps

The Human Body

Longest Hair

takes too long

Tallest Man

bricks???

Most Number of Bones Broken

check out foot thing

Stretchiest Skin

Loudest Scream

If we do the bones thing? two records at the same time???

SPORTS AND GAMES

MOST NUMBER OF CONSECUTIVE FOOTY PASSES

√√√ easy!

LONGEST TENNIS GAME

HEAVIEST BENCH PRESS

bricks???

LONGEST TIME HOLDING BREATH (UNDERWATER)

??????

"I marked some things," he says. "Forget the stupid onion. There's heaps of cool stuff in here." He waves a finger at Ronnie. "If you want to be famous for eating your vegies, mate, you go ahead. Me and Nath have got bigger plans." He glances at me. "Right?"

I think about getting up there at assembly. I imagine Mr Stipanov calling my name, the whole school clapping. I think about my picture in the paper, my name in the book. I remember how it felt to whiz past Josh Tuttle's classroom, even though he didn't happen to be there at the time.

I'm not ready for the onion.

I nod. "Yeah."

Ronnie shrugs and tosses the onion from hand to hand. "It's your funeral."

At the time, I think he's joking.

CHAPTER 7
FIFTY-TWO TINY BONES

We start with fastest furniture. The junk pile near the bike ramp gives us lots to choose from, though most of it looks pretty dodgy. I try not to look at the smashed-up ramp while Weasel picks through the rubbish. He has this idea that we should take the engine out of an old lawnmower and attach it to the mouldy old couch with ockie straps.

"These things are handy," he says, snapping one back and forth. "This is going to be cool."

Then he realises that he doesn't know how to

get the engine out, and that the couch doesn't have any wheels.

He stands back and looks thoughtful for a minute, then grins.

Next thing I know, I'm sitting in a shopping trolley, on a couch cushion, while Weasel straps an entire lawnmower to the front.

"No worries," he says, snapping an ockie strap into place. It's not exactly fastest furniture, not really, but according to Weasel we've got all the key elements: a couch and some wheels and an engine, and me. Somewhere along the way, we decide to ignore the fact that the engine isn't exactly attached to the wheels, and that the couch has become kind of irrelevant, apart from giving me something squishy to sit on.

Like I said, we are all class.

Science Boy reckons it's dumb. He says that even if we get any speed up, it won't count. He jabs a finger at the book and raises his eyebrows.

FURNITURE DRIVEN BY MAKESHIFT MOTORISED ENGINE

"*Driven by*?" he says. "*Furniture*?"

"*Makeshift*!" Weasel counters, and yanks on the mower's starter cord.

We're not really doing it yet, not going for it. It would be pointless up here, because it's all rough and rocky. We need somewhere flat and smooth. Somewhere fast. But first we need to practise a bit, make sure everything works.

Don't tell me we don't learn from our mistakes.

Of course, the engine doesn't start, because the lawnmower is junk, and that's why it's on a rubbish dump in the first place.

Science Boy would probably have told us that if we'd asked. But we don't. We just tell him to stand by and hold the camera.

Weasel pulls the starter cord about a hundred times, and each time the trolley edges forward on the sloping ground. By the time he gives up, the trolley is rolling. All by itself.

Only not alone, because it's got me inside it. Also rolling. Right over the side of the hill.

The last thing I see before I go over is Weasel's panicked face as he turns to run after me. With no hope at all of catching up.

Then I see sky, and prickle bushes, and rocky ground, each one more painful than the last.

Weasel and Ronnie find me on my back halfway down, in the middle of a bush. When I try to move, the points of a thousand tiny needles press further into my skin.

In one hand, Weasel is clutching a frayed starter cord.

"No good, mate," he says. "It's stuffed."

"Tell me about it," I groan.

Next, I try holding my breath underwater.

Weasel generously offers to help me keep my head

in the bucket, so I can "push past my fear", and I stupidly agree to let him.

Later, he says we should probably have decided on a signal, something I could do to tell him I was really serious about needing to breathe.

I tell him that I'm fairly sure spluttering and waving your arms around like a mad chicken is the international code for *Stop holding my head underwater, I'm drowning!*

He tells me I was only under for fifty-six seconds, not even one-eighth of the record, and there's no way I was drowning. What I needed to do, he says, was relax.

I ask him if he would like me to hold his head underwater for a while, and he politely declines.

Ronnie turns the camera off and pats his pocket again. "Did you know," he says, "that if you chop onions underwater, you don't cry?"

I offer to make him cry, and he politely declines.

"Milk bottles," Weasel says, pointing to a picture of a boy, an oar, and a raft made of plastic bottles lashed together with rope.

CATEGORY: TRAVEL AND TRANSPORT
RECORD: FASTEST FIFTY METRES BY
MILK-BOTTLE RAFT

Ockie straps and glue. Bottles from the recycling bin. A paddle from Dad's old kayak.

No worries.

Of course, they won't let us do it at the pool, so Ronnie paces the length of it, then marks out the distance along the river.

About halfway, with Ronnie and Weasel screaming at me from the bank, I plough my paddle into a jellyfish. It sticks to the end, its guts hanging out, looking as disgusting as anything I've ever seen. I try to keep paddling, but every time I move, revolting goop sprays everywhere. I shake the paddle, trying to fling the thing back into the river, and that's when it flies off and lands in my lap.

I do what anyone would do. I yell and throw

myself backwards. And that's when I discover that milk-bottle rafts aren't built for balance.

A split second later I'm in the river, under the flipped-over raft, with oozing jellyfish guts filling the water around me.

I tell myself to relax and push through my fear. But then I decide I'd rather freak out and panic.

When my head breaks the surface, I can't see for a second. At least not clearly. There's a thin film of jellyfish in front of my eyes, like a curtain of snot.

And then I hear the applause and see the crowd. A birthday party of kids, just spilled out of two mini-vans, all standing on the bank of the river, staring. A wall of parents behind them, with camcorders.

As I drag the so-called raft up onto the bank, the kids crowd around me.

"That was cool!" one of them says.

"I want a jellyfish idiot for *my* party!" says another.

"He eats onions too," says Ronnie. "Underwater."

"Coool!" says a kid behind me.

"Hey," I say, wiping the last of the jellyfish snot off my face. "You should probably try out for *Neighbours*."

The next day, Weasel offers to stretch me on a rack. "*Most Rapid Growth*," he says. "We could tie bricks to your feet and hang you from the monkey bars."

In the background, Science Boy is shaking his head wildly. But it's okay. Even I'm not stupid enough to let Weasel tie bricks to my legs.

I *am* stupid enough to let him talk me into trying to roll one kilometre in under eight minutes (gravel rash and a serious head-spin). Then I'm crazy enough to believe he'll be a good partner for most number of consecutive footy passes (thumb bent back at disturbing angle, followed by blood nose). Then I'm insane enough to try balancing thirty-nine books on my head (twelve cracked spines – the books, not mine; one cracking headache – mine; and a painful dent across my toes where *Amazing World Records* hit the deck).

In two days, I'm idiot enough to try a total of twenty-six different amazing world record attempts, each one more stupid and impossible than the last.

By number twenty-seven, I'm battered and bruised enough that Weasel's starting to suggest I could try for "most bones broken".

"It's 433," he says. "That's in a lifetime, but you could do a shorter version, over a week. You could do fifty, easy."

I stare at him.

"Did you know," he says, "that there are twenty-six bones in each foot? If you just got each one – methodically, you know, with a hammer – you'd be done. And you'd still have the use of your hands."

"Bonus," I mutter.

He's not serious about the hammer, of course. At least, I don't think so. Maybe he's just trying to soften me up, threatening me with having fifty-two tiny bones broken so his next idea will sound tame in comparison.

CHAPTER 8
WHEN COCKROACHES ATTACK

"Bugs?" I stare down at the bucket. There's a lid, so I can't see inside, not clearly. But I can make out what looks like hundreds of tiny shapes scuttling around, beating up and down the sides.

Shapes with wings.

And antennae.

Cockroaches.

"No way," Ronnie and I say together. "No way."

Weasel lifts the lid, and already one of the disgusting little heads is pushing its way up, trying to scramble out over the top.

They're not just cockroaches, but the giant flying kind. Thousands of them live in the pipe down here behind the bike shed.

"Two minutes," Weasel says. "Two minutes. Thirty-seven cockroaches. No worries."

"I am *not* eating cockroaches," I say.

Weasel laughs. "They're good for you," he says. "Full of fibre."

I bend down and peer into the disgusting mess of bugs. Not because I'm going to do it, but just for a look. Just to get the feel of it. Just so I can remind myself how much I don't want to do this.

That's when the cockroaches attack.

One cockroach, anyway.

It's like it sees my big moon-face coming at it and just launches itself into space. It takes off like a helicopter, its wings buzzing and clicking, its disgusting antennae scanning from side to side. It comes straight at me, like I'm a landing pad.

It's on my face, crawling and feeling and tracking

its revolting little legs everywhere, brushing my cheeks with its wings.

"Aggh!" I stagger backwards, yelling, and that's when it finds my mouth.

I bite down without thinking, just trying to shut my mouth, to keep it out, but already it's half-in, half-out, and my teeth close over something disgusting.

And crunchy.

"One!" screams Weasel. "That's it, mate. Exactly!"

"You've got a leg in your mouth!" Ronnie yells.

Down the point of my nose, I watch a one-and-a-half-legged cockroach take off and head towards the pipe. Other roaches spill out of the bucket, running and flying after the first one, climbing on top of each other to get away.

I spit, and splutter, and wipe my mouth with the back of my hand.

Then I turn to Ronnie.

I know what he's thinking.

"Behold the onion," he says. "How it tastes way, way better than kamikaze cockroaches."

I look around me, at the bucket and the escaping cockroaches, and Weasel, who's torn between chasing the cockroaches and falling over laughing.

I think about the splitting wood and the sofa springs and the welding iron. I think about the prickle bush and the near-drowning and the jellyfish snot.

I rub my knee, and my arm, and the bump on my head, and every cut and bruise on my body throbs like a drumbeat.

I don't look at Weasel. I pick cockroach from my teeth and hold out one hand. "Give me the onion," I say.

Ronnie nods. He tosses it to me and his face goes serious.

"One minute and thirty-five seconds," he says. "One whole onion." He pats his backpack. "I've got more, just in case. Not that they're going to try and escape or anything." He shoots a look at Weasel. "Since they don't have wings. Or legs."

Weasel shrugs. "Do what you want," he says. "I just don't know how we got from amazing bike jumps to eating onions."

I snort. "How about cockroaches? How did we get from amazing bike jumps to eating cockroaches?"

Weasel looks annoyed. "At least cockroaches are interesting. At least they're unusual."

"Onions are unusual," I say. "Right, Ronnie?"

I'm not sure if I'm trying to convince Weasel or myself.

"Right." Ronnie rummages in his backpack for a second and pulls something out. "Here. You'll need these."

"Swimming goggles?"

"To stop you crying. You know, from the juice."

Weasel rolls his eyes. "It just gets better, doesn't it?"

I ignore him and start pulling the peel off the onion. Halfway through, my eyes start to water and I snap the goggles on over my head.

Weasel turns away in disgust.

Ronnie turns the camera on and starts counting down.

CHAPTER 9
BEHOLD THE ONION

The first time, I don't even get halfway. Just biting into the thing is a shock. Juice sprays everywhere and pieces of onion slice into the sides of my cheeks. My whole mouth is on fire. I shake my head and stop. Ronnie throws me a water bottle, then another onion. Weasel's on his hands and knees, staring hopefully into the pipe.

"I can always get more cockroaches," he says.

The second time is better. The inside of my mouth is going numb so it doesn't burn as much. The smell is brutal, though. Either the goggles don't seal properly, or the juice is so toxic it doesn't matter. I get through about half before I start spitting it out, my eyes streaming with tears.

It's the third attempt when it all comes together.

I decide to just do it. I sucker the edges of the goggles in hard around my eye sockets. I get Ronnie to choose the smallest onion he can find that's still big enough for the record. I tell myself that pain is good. Onion juice, too. I close my eyes and imagine I'm biting into a juicy, green apple.

Bite and chew. Bite and chew. Nothing else matters.

I can't taste it. Can't feel it.

I'm an eating machine.

Halfway through the onion, I'm picking up speed. And I'm not going to stop. My goggles are fogging up, but I see Weasel turn from the pipe. He forgets about cockroaches. He stares at me, then darts over to Ronnie.

"Are you getting this?" he says.

Ronnie nods, his face set.

Bite and chew. Bite and chew.

Flecks of onion spray everywhere. I scoop up the chunks – have to eat everything or it won't count – and keep going.

About the one-minute mark, I start having doubts. Maybe I should do this another day, when I have an empty stomach. Or maybe this isn't good for me. Maybe it's damaging my guts or something. Maybe I'm going blind. Maybe we should go back and try the bike thing again. Maybe I could eat a cockroach instead. Maybe thirty-seven isn't that many after all. My brain tries everything to get me to stop.

That's when Weasel starts screaming. "Nearly there, Nath! Come on!" He's in my face, hands flapping wildly.

I wave him away and chow down. I tell my brain to shut up, and just keep chewing. A few more bites, then one big swallow. Ronnie's hopping on one foot, jiggling the camera, counting down:

"*Eighteen!*

"*Seventeen!*

"*Sixteen!*"

I'm so close. I'm chewing and swallowing and I can almost taste the record, mixed in with all the onion. There's no splintering wood, no spiky metal. I'm going to make it. I can see my picture in *Amazing World Records*, grinning out at kids all over the world. I can see the assembly, the stage, Josh Tuttle's envious face.

Josh Tuttle's *leering* face.

I can actually see it.

Coming around the corner.

And someone else.

And someone else.

Wearing AFL shorts and hand-passing a footy between them.

I gag on the last bit of onion.

Weasel turns and Ronnie turns, and Josh Tuttle grins and looks around him.

"Nice look, mate," he says, waving a hand at the goggles and my drooling, onion-flecked mouth. "What are you trying out for, the Idiot Olympics?"

"*Two* ...

"*One* ...

"Zero."

Ronnie lowers the camera.

Weasel looks at me hopefully, but he knows already. We all do.

There's a big chunk of onion still in my mouth, which is on fire again all of a sudden.

The Josh Tuttle effect, I'll call it.

I shake my head and spit the onion out onto the grass in front of me.

Josh Tuttle peers at me. "Mate," he says. "You've got onion on your face. And ... some kind of brown stuff in your teeth." He leans in closer. "Gross. What *is* that?"

"Nothing." I grab at the water bottle.

Josh notices the book, then, lying splattered with onion juice off to one side. "Is that a library book?" He lunges for it. "You are so busted!"

I let him take it. I don't care about the book. I'm too busy waving at Ronnie to get the camera away, out of sight, before Josh and his mates realise the entire Idiot Olympics is available on film.

Ronnie tries to cram the camera under his jacket, but just then Mr Marshall comes around the corner. He looks around him, at the bucket, and the onions, and the goggles, and takes a step towards Ronnie. "What are you kids doing?" he says. He reaches for the camera. "Hand it over."

Josh passes the book off quickly to a guy behind him, who shoves it in his bag. "It wasn't us," he says. "We were just practising. Footy. You know, for the school team."

Mr Marshall growls. "You don't practise footy behind the bike shed. With onions and goggles and" – he peers at me – "other brown stuff."

"Not them," Josh argues. "Us." He points around him at the others, at their footy gear.

"Doesn't matter." Mr Marshall scowls. "You can't be here in the holidays. So clear off, the lot of you."

Josh and the others mutter a bit, then head off around the corner and out of sight. Weasel grabs the bucket and Ronnie scrambles to zip up his backpack.

"Could I have the camera back?" he asks.

Mr Marshall shakes his head. "I'm going to have a look at this first. See what you've been up to."

Ronnie turns pale. "Mum's going to kill me."

Weasel digs me in the ribs and points to the grass near the pipe. Josh has left his footy behind. "We could try the passing again," Weasel says. "Come on. Just one last go."

I rub a finger across my bruised nose. "Forget it. It's over. No more bike jumps and shopping trolleys and jellyfish snot. It was a stupid idea in the first place. *Amazing World Records*. Yeah, right."

Mr Marshall's busy staring at the camera, fiddling with buttons, but he looks up then, with a weird expression on his face.

"*Amazing World Records*? You guys ... hang on – you trying to break a record?"

"Yeah, just a few."

He takes a step towards me. "What did you do? Bike jumps? I bet you did bike jumps." He pauses. "Skateboard! The railing thing – right?"

I shuffle my feet. "Yeah, kind of. We tried heaps

of stuff. But it doesn't matter. We stuffed everything up. Totally."

Something comes across Mr Marshall's face then – a half-smile, creeping, like the beginning of an idea.

"How many? How many things?" He waves the camera. "Did you film everything?"

Ronnie nods. "It's my mum's. She–"

Mr Marshall waves him silent. "Boys," he says. "Come with me. We need to talk."

CHAPTER 10
A BOY NEEDS
A TROPHY

I'd drop my trophy on Josh Tuttle's foot if I could, but he's too far away. Everyone is far away because I'm up here on the stage, on my own, while a movie of moments from my thirty-one officially approved world record attempts plays on the enormous screen behind me.

It's a miracle of editing. There are no crashes or near-impalings, just frame after frame of me pointing my bike like an arrow, fearlessly sticking my face into a bucket of cockroaches, turning a shopping trolley and a lawnmower into an incredible speed-machine. Even Janie Parsons looks impressed.

"Well, children," Mr Stipanov begins, "I think you'll agree that this is quite an achievement. It's a real credit to the school, to have an *Amazing World Record* holder among us."

I look down at the trophy and smile. You don't normally get a trophy, just your name in the book and a certificate. But Mr Stipanov and Mr Marshall insisted. "A boy needs a trophy," they said.

They were grinning like maniacs.

After we'd cleaned up the onion, Mr Marshall marched us to Mr Stipanov's office. There he was, sitting at his desk even though it was the holidays, thinking up new ideas for merit awards and waiting to yell at kids who were caught on school property.

We were so busted.

Except not.

Mr Marshall and Mr Stipanov whispered for a few minutes, then Mr Stipanov pulled a heavy book down off the shelf. He flipped through it, then came out and asked us a bunch of questions – *how long, how far, how many, how tragic?* He checked out all my bruises and nodded, with a strange gleam in his eye.

Then he patted me on the back and made a phone call.

"Yes, yes, I can. Yes, that's right. Exactly. I know. Well, I realise. Stipanov. Yes, and Marshall. These boys … uh-huh. Yes, we do. On film. Can do. Sure. Excellent."

After he put the phone down, he pulled a crumpled old photo out of his wallet. In it, two ratty looking kids were standing next to a 44-gallon drum. The drum looked kind of banged up, and so did one of the kids. But they were both grinning. And looking strangely familiar.

Mr Stipanov high fived Mr Marshall, and winked at me. He held up the book he'd taken down from the shelf. *"Amazing World Records,"* he said. "Longest downhill barrel roll. I broke my nose. It was worth it, though."

I stared at them. "But you … you're not in the book," I said. "Are you?"

I ran my finger down the index to "Travel and

Transport: Longest Barrel Roll" and flipped to the right page.

NOBUKO EGAWA, AGE 13, 1964: SEVENTY-THREE METRES

A Japanese girl smiled out from the photo. Her nose looked intact.

Mr Stipanov sighed. "Sixteen minutes," he said. "Sixteen minutes we held that record. We never even made it into print."

"We were going to try again," Mr Marshall said, "but we couldn't find a longer slope."

"And my parents were kind of cranky about the nose thing," Mr Stipanov added.

"We *are* in the book, though." Mr Marshall turned to the back. "Here." He tapped an entry in the middle of the page, and there they were:

CATEGORY: RECORDS ABOUT RECORDS
RECORD: SHORTEST PERIOD OF TIME HOLDING AMAZING WORLD RECORD

HELD BY: CHRISTOPHER STIPANOV AND JOHN MARSHALL, AGE 12, 1964: SIXTEEN MINUTES

He turned to me. "This is where yours will go, too."

It was a new record, he said. Nothing like this had ever happened before. Because most people don't have our speed. Most people plan for ages to try for a record. They consider every angle; they think about safety, timing, the laws of physics.

Ronnie shook his head and mouthed, "I told you so."

He didn't care, though. None of us did. Because we were going to be in *Amazing World Records*.

And also on stage.

I look down at the plaque on the front of the trophy. It's so cool how Mr Stipanov talked them into leaving the word *unsuccessful* out of it.

"It's irrelevant," he said. "The number's the thing. The sheer perseverance of these young lads. The commitment, the stickability, the absolute … yes, exactly. Thank you."

That's how I ended up here, in front of the whole school, with a trophy the size of a small horse, engraved in gold lettering with the words: *Most Number of Amazing World Record Attempts In 48 Hours.*

We know the record won't last long. Once it's in the book, all kinds of reckless idiots will start going for it. They'll be cramming the attempts in, half-killing themselves, grabbing fistfuls of cockroaches and scorpions as they whiz past in their rocket-powered bathtubs full of snakes on their way to a near-impaling.

It doesn't matter. We made it in, and that's what counts.

I grin out at Weasel and Ronnie and they give me the big thumbs up.

The microphone crackles as Mr Stipanov begins a new announcement. I go to leave the stage, but he waves at me to stay.

"Wonderfully responsible," Mr Stipanov says. "Showing a real commitment to books and literacy." He holds up a small square of cardboard and motions to someone down the back.

Turns out some kid has won a merit award for "Services to the Library", sub-category: "Rescuing Abused Library Books Without Thought For Personal Gain".

There's movement at the back, and someone stands and starts picking his way towards the front.

It's someone small and wiry, someone who really, really doesn't want to come up here. But he has no choice, because everyone's waiting, and clapping their slow, half-hearted claps, and the air is just opening up to let him through.

Josh Tuttle reaches the stage and holds out his hand for his craptacular square of cardboard.

The newspaper photographer moves around in front, and Mr Stipanov motions to Weasel and Ronnie to come up. The three of us crowd in together, and the photographer frowns.

"Just try and squeeze in," he tells Josh. "Maybe sit down on the side there. And hold up your ... library award thing."

In the newspaper tomorrow there will be a front-page photo with the headline:

Amazing Boys Take on the World.

There'll be me and Weasel and Ronnie, grinning our faces off, holding a trophy the size of a small horse. And there'll be Josh Tuttle, whose tiny shadow doesn't even make a blip on the pictures of our amazing amazingness flashing behind us. Josh Tuttle, library wonder boy, holding up his smiley-stickered cardboard and screwing up his face like a howler monkey as Weasel digs him invisibly in the ribs.

Sucked in to that kid.

HAVE YOU BEEN STRUCK YET?
MORE LIGHTNING STRIKES!

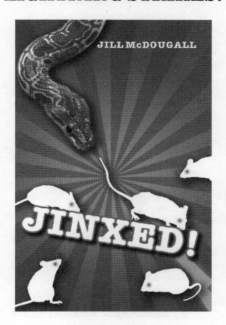

JINXED!

Jinx loves jokes. (Some of her best friends are jokes – ha, ha.) But an accident involving a pet python and broken glass is no joking matter.

Jinx needs to make some fast cash ... really fast.

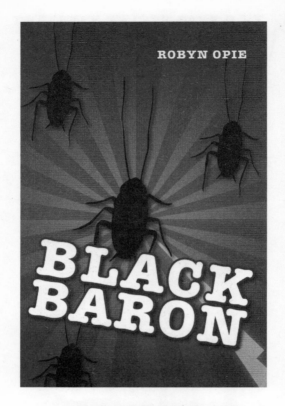

ROBYN OPIE

BLACK BARON

BLACK BARON

Black Baron, the best racing
cockroach ever, has won again!
Jake is on top of the world.
Until Mum discovers Black
Baron under Jake's bed.
Can Jake save Black
Baron from certain death?

JOHN PARKER

SUCKED IN

SUCKED IN

When Zainey buys an eye,
Dan thinks it's a total
rip-off – a useless joke.
But this eye is no joke.
This eye is after blood.